MURDERED AT MIDNIGHT

A Gruesome Horror Story

JUSTIN MEAD

PAGE PUBLISHING
Conneaut Lake, PA

First originally published by Page Publishing 2024

ISBN 979-8-89157-323-9 (pbk)
ISBN 979-8-89157-341-3 (digital)

Printed in the United States of America

CHAPTER 1

THE FUN STARTS

The sun shines, making the woods glow brightly. The woods in Idaho are peaceful and quiet with no sound. Deep within the woods, trees of dark wood surround a cracked tombstone. RIP is the only thing engraved on it. A loud roar of a sports car is heard waking up the trees, making the crows fly away. The ground under the tombstone shakes as if an earthquake was happening. The tombstone breaks with each piece hitting the rough terrain then dissolves into nothingness. The ground shakes once again, but this time, a disfigured hand reaches out. The ground then splits open with smoke filling the air. A loud roar from an unknown creature is heard so loud that the passing car's passenger window breaks. The glass shatters and cuts a beautiful blonde woman.

"Aah, what the fuck. Danny, what the fuck! Are you fucking kidding me!" yells the beautiful blonde named Lola. She starts touching her face and then wipes off the glass on her lap.

"What the fuck just happened?" asks the driver whose name is Danny. Danny is this big bulk guy. He has short brown hair, big muscles, and always wears this green unique sweater that has a big yellow smiley face in the middle.

"The fucking window, Danny!" yells Lola. "Aren't you fucking mad?" she asks.

Danny ignores her and continues his focus on the road.

"You just bought the fucking car, and now some stupid pebble or rock just fucking shattered the window!" Lola screams, this time right in Danny's face.

Danny continues to remain calm and starts to drive slowly.

"That wasn't any rock, fool. Are you telling me you guys didn't hear that odd sound?" says Danny's younger brother, Bill.

Bill is this slim guy who has crazy curly brown hair and wears a dark blue varsity jacket. Bill is sitting in the back with two other girls. He's in the middle. The girl on the right is also blonde, but she wears a ton of makeup, making her look like a Barbie doll, while the girl on the left has dark brown hair and wears red glasses. The two blondes are both wearing matching green sweatshirts while the girl on the left is in a gray turtleneck. All three girls wear blue jeans and matching black sneakers.

"A noise?" Danny asks as he briefly looks at his brother in the rearview mirror. "Nah, that was the music on the radio. Must've had some static or something, man."

"What fucking music, Danny? The radio has been off for a long while now," Bill mutters.

He then turns to his left and just starts staring out the window. The girl on the left locks eyes with Bill. When he looks up and notices, she quickly looks down on her lap and starts reading the book she had opened up. She reads silently to herself and shuts everyone around her out. Danny starts to pick up the speed a little bit. He turns and looks at Lola who's touching her face again.

"We are almost there, my love," Danny says.

Lola just ignores him and continues touching around her face.

"Babe, the right side of your cheek is cut."

Lola starts touching her face frantically until she finds the wound. She opens the glove box and takes out a Kleenex and wipes her cheek. The car comes to a stop, parking in front of an old yellow two-story cabin that's hidden in the woods. The sun shines so bright it hits the cabin, making the yellow deteriorating wood more glorious and beautiful to the eye. Danny's car has parked next to this gray Ferrari. Bill eyeballs the car and smiles. Everyone exits the vehicle. Danny kisses Lola and then runs up to the cabin. The door swings open with a tall man covered in tattoos now presenting himself in front of Danny. The man is shirtless, sweating, and wears a green baseball hat, but it's backward. The man smiles at Danny and chuckles.

"Awww, come on, Patriot. You need to put on a fucking shirt, man. You gonna scare October and Girl over there, you fuck," Danny says to the tall shirtless man.

The man laughs and then walks up to Danny. "Alright, and which one is October?" Patriot asks as he eyeballs all the girls standing by the two cars. Danny points to the girl with red glasses who's standing next to Bill reading her book. Patriot laughs again.

"And trust me, bro, she isn't interested in you. The one who kinda looks like a slut might be. Her name is Girl," Danny says.

Patriot looks at Girl and smiles at her. He then waves, trying to get her attention, but she's just ignoring him.

"Girl? What kind of stupid fucking name is that?" Patriot asks as he continues to wave, trying to get Girl's attention.

"I have no fucking clue. Girlenza is her real name, we just call her Girl for short."

"Well, I'm gonna fuck her, bro. She's a total baddie. Just my type," Patriot says. He laughs and then hugs Danny. After three seconds, Danny pushes him off.

"You fucking nasty sweaty pig. Bro, go put on a fucking T-shirt."

They both laugh together insanely while the girls all look at each other and then at them.

"I missed you, man. Nice shitty Ford by the way."

"Fuck you, Patriot. A car is a fucking car," Danny says, laughing. "I miss you too. I've just been so fucking busy. Lola and I took our relationship to the next level. I asked her to marry me last Friday, and she said yes. So we are now engaged. Also I've been stuck babysitting my stupid, lowlife, fuckup, dumbass, and retarded little brother," Danny says as he turns and looks at Bill for a second.

"It's cool, bro. I'm just fucking with you, ya know. Just yanking ya cock. Mike and Joint are inside. We got here first and also found the hidden key under the mat. We also helped ourselves to some lemonade and cocaine," Patriot says as he turns around and walks back inside the cabin.

Patriot has this tattoo of a bald eagle carrying an American flag, which covers his entire back. Danny admires the artwork. He then calls for everyone and waves them inside. Bill, trying to be a gentleman, carries October's black duffel bag. He struggles a bit but manages not to make himself look foolish.

"What the fuck do you have in here, beautiful? Books?" Bill asks as he tries to catch up to her, but she's walking fast.

"Just my stuff, ya know. Books, weed, and clothes. Better not drop my bag. If you do, no reward, tough guy," October says to Bill, not even looking at him.

"What's the reward?" Bill asks, smiling.

"Fuck around and find out," October says as she looks at Bill and licks her lips.

She makes it to the cabin and holds the door open for Bill who's blushing. His face is as red as the blood dripping down Lola's cheek. The room everyone enters is a large living room. The first thing that catches everyone's eye is the large stone fireplace that's lit with the fire warming the room. A double-barrel shotgun is hung proudly above the fireplace next to a picture of an old bald man who's wearing green suspenders. There's one big green couch in the center, a boom box on a small wooden table next to the couch, and a rocking chair in the right corner.

Straight ahead is the kitchen, and to the right is a staircase that leads upstairs to all the bedrooms. Bill throws October's duffel bag on the couch and then walks over to the fireplace, admiring the shotgun. He then stares at the picture of the bald man. The man in the picture is holding the same shotgun that's hung up.

"Grandpa was fucking weird. But he sure loved hunting and that shotgun," Danny says as he then walks over to Bill.

"Yeah, I miss that old fuck. He took us in when our parents passed. It's sad how you see them and speak to them and then one day a car accident occurs and then they are both dead. Luckily, Gramps got to die of old age. Old fucker is a legend though," Bill says emotionally. He then turns around and grabs October's duffel bag.

Danny just stands there looking at the picture while flashbacks of good memories play in his head.

"So do we all get our own rooms or what?" Bill asks Danny.

Danny smiles at the picture of his grandpa. He then turns around to face Bill. "There's only three bedrooms upstairs. I get the master bedroom with my fiancée. You and Joint can share a room, Patriot gets the couch with Mike, and October and Girl can share the last room which also has two beds," Danny says, answering Bill's question.

"Share a room with Joint?" Bill asks with a puzzled expression.

"That motherfucker gonna end up sleeping on the floor with how stupid he about to get tonight. That crazy fucking stoner, hippie, whatever the fuck he is."

Bill and Danny laugh. Bill then goes upstairs with October following him closely. Bill gets to the second to the last step and then turns to October. "Would you wanna maybe share a room?" Bill asks her.

October's eyes widened with a smile also showing. She then starts to blush. "Just maybe, Billy," she says back to him. She then grabs her duffel bag from Bill and proceeds up the stairs.

Bill scoots to the side allowing her to pass. She makes it to the top and then looks down at him.

"Hey, October, I get really, really cold at night. Some cuddles and some love would definitely help with that."

"Just maybe, Billy," she says again. She blows Bill a kiss and then walks into the room on the far left and shuts the door. A locking sound is heard, which makes Bill laugh.

"Just don't call me Billy, I fucking hate that," Bill says as he goes back downstairs.

Laughs are heard from the kitchen. Bill notices that everyone has left the living room, so he leaves too, walking straight into the kitchen. The kitchen is massive. A long dining room table is placed in the middle with Girl, Lola, and Danny sitting in the chairs that surround it. The kitchen has an oven, a long sink surrounded by cabinets, and a big walk-in pantry all on the left side. The right side is a bar area with stools, the table, and, of course, all the drinks which hang proudly on a shelf above.

Patriot, who's now wearing a black T-shirt, is behind the bar table acting as a bartender to these two guys who are sitting on the stools drinking a tall glass of beer. The guy on the left has long brown hair, wears a gray beanie, and a short-sleeved tie-dye shirt. He's also smoking a joint, and he's covered in tattoos that fill up both arms, his left hand, and neck. The tattoo on his left hand is a colorful rose with a skull on the right side getting punched by brass knuckles. The guy also has a beard that makes him look like a terrorist. Bill walks to the bar, heading toward the two guys. On the bar table, he sees a small glass bong, a few empty beer bottles, and what looks like a rock of cocaine just sitting there.

As Bill walks over, all the guys at the bar turn and look at him and laugh. The guy on the right gets up and runs straight at Bill. This guy is wearing the same varsity jacket as Bill, basically matching him. This guy appears to be very young, like midtwenties, clean-shaven, has short hair, and he is black. He reaches Bill and gives him a huge hug, wrapping his arms around Bill and then lifting him into the air. They smile and laugh at each other as the man spins Bill around twice and then drops him to the ground.

"Mike, I fucking missed you so much."

"That sounded kinda gay, Bill. Maybe tone that down a bit while I'm here."

They both start to laugh. Shortly after, everyone starts to laugh.

"About fucking time y'all. Let's get this fucking party fucking started!" Mike yells out loud.

The girls start to giggle as Patriot pours four shots. Patriot looks up and sees Girl staring him down. He lifts up one of the shot glasses and raises it up in the air.

"Shots! Shots! Shots!" Patriot yells in excitement. He then takes his shot and slams the empty glass onto the bar table.

"Seems like you guys have been partying already, huh? Already high, drunk, and on coke, huh?" Danny yells back, looking at Mike and Patriot.

"Party starts when you all get here. We've been waiting. I'm not drunk yet. I definitely need like ten more beers and such. Mike and Joint are just high as fuck, like outta their fucking minds. No one has done any coke yet," Patriot says, answering Danny who's kind of acting like a party pooper.

Mike walks back to the bar, and Patriot hands him a shot glass. The girls both get up and head toward the bar too, leaving Danny alone at the table. Girl grabs a shot glass and then smiles at the man with the unique hand tattoo.

"Joint, you fucking stoner. I'm glad you made it. I missed you. I've been thinking about you," Girl says, smiling at the man, licking her red lips, showing him her tongue.

Joint smiles back and takes his shot. He then takes a hit off the joint and passes it to Girl. She takes it, takes a hit, and passes it back to Joint.

Danny, watching everyone laugh and drink, gets up and walks toward the bar. Everyone starts to laugh and cheer. Danny takes a shot and quickly drinks it.

Patriot starts to pour everyone a shot. Everyone grabs their glass and raises it up and then drinks it. The kitchen becomes loud, full of laughs, cries, and smoke from the marijuana.

The girls leave the bar as October calls them out of the kitchen so they could jam out to some music in the living room. Danny follows so he can be with Lola, leaving Mike, Joint, Patriot, and Bill at the bar. The cocaine rock is still untouched but eyed by Mike and Bill.

"So who brought the snow?" asks Bill.

Patriot starts to dig in his right pocket. He then pulls out a small razor blade and a quarter. He uses the coin to press and crush the cocaine.

"It's Mike's. Joint doesn't like anything else besides weed, so he won't partake. I also pitched in for this, so enjoy, fuckers, enjoy," Patriot says as he then uses the razor blade and makes four lines out of the crushed cocaine.

Mike, already holding a one-hundred-dollar bill, uses it to snort one line. Mike wipes his nose, grinning, and hands the rolled bill to Patriot. Patriot does two lines. After he finishes the second one, he drops the dollar on the table and runs around in circles all around the bar, yelling and stomping.

"Fuck, that was so fucking good! I feel like a motherfucking king! King fucking Patriot!" Patriot yells and stomps around some more. He stops after five minutes and then walks back to the bar and sits down on a stool.

Bill laughs. "You are a dumb fucking maniac. Are you trying to piss my brother off? Like fuck, man," Bill says as he stares down Patriot.

Patriot looks back at Bill, angered. "You and Danny got so lucky with this. Got yourselves a nice fucking house, cabin, whatever you wanna fucking call it. Whatever. It's nice and warm, and I feel lit as fuck being here. So party, Billy. It's your fucking house cabin thing. Fucking party, get lit, get high, get drunk, and do some fucking blow, man. Maybe fuck October, I don't know, but party, you lucky fuck. None of us are lucky, you stupid rich fucks," Patriot says, slurring his words like a drunk fool.

Bill laughs because he tries to take nothing too seriously. Bill grabs the rolled-up one-hundred-dollar bill.

"You know what, Patriot?" Bill asks. Patriot just looks up at him. Everything in his point of view is blurry. "You didn't lose your fucking parents and then your grandparents too shortly after! Fuck you, man, fuck you!" Bill yells.

"I ain't lucky—only fucking Danny is, man. He's the one who got to take over this place when Grandpa died. I didn't get shit that's because I was never there. Motherfucker even put that in his will too. Being the family's disappointment comes with hella perks. Here you are though talking like you actually fucking know something. You are never around."

Bill snorts the last line on the table and then drops the one-hundred-dollar bill.

"Danny's better than me. He's getting married, he has a nice job, he has a two-story house, and now a two-story cabin. Fuck my brother. You know what I got? A losing record in football, drug addiction, sex addiction, depression, and a fucking criminal record when all I did was piss in a park's sandbox drunk as fuck. Yeah, that's what the fuck I got," Bill says.

Patriot starts to nod his head. He then stares Bill down. "Danny's my best fucking friend. He's been there for me through thick and fucking thin. I don't appreciate you talking shit on him when all he does is watch over and protect your sorry ass. You being a dumb fuckup, that's all on you, man," Patriot says back to Bill.

Bill, angered, gets up and takes the joint out of Joint's mouth. He then flips Patriot off and leaves the kitchen. Patriot starts to laugh.

"Fuck off, Patriot, he's been through enough. Let the kid fucking vent, man. Why do you gotta be a fucking dick all the time?" Joint says as he dogs out Patriot.

Patriot laughs again and pours himself another shot. Before he can drink it, Mike snatches it, drinks it, flips Patriot off, and then leaves the kitchen, following Bill.

"Whatever, Mike! Have fun and lighten up, you young dumb fucker!" Patriot yells.

Patriot grabs a full beer that was left on the table and starts to chug it. Joint pull out another joint and lights it up. As he inhales the marijuana, music can be heard loudly coming out of the living room. Lola and Girl are heard laughing and cheering out loud

"You wanna join in on whatever the fuck is going on in there?" Patriot asks Joint. Joint laughs and inhales more of the marijuana

"Naw, I'd rather stay right here and get as high as I possibly fucking can, man," Joint says back to Patriot who then pours two shots. They take them instantly, and then start passing the joint back and forth, causing the kitchen to be full of smoke.

CHAPTER 2

MURDERED AT MIDNIGHT

The sun is gone. Darkness is everywhere with the only light in the sky being the stars. They don't shine bright; in fact, in this part of the woods, nothing seems to shine at all at night. Not the moon, which is full tonight, and not even the damn porch light. The woods aren't quiet tonight as loud music is heard coming from inside the cabin. In the living room, the boom box plays "I'm Still Standing" by Elton John. The music blasts loudly, shaking up the cabin and every room inside.

Girl and Lola are dancing around the living room with beers in their hands, drinking, laughing, and having the time of their lives. October is sitting in the rocking chair, drinking a beer, and looking at

Bill who seems sad. Bill is just sitting on the couch next to Mike, smoking the joint he took.

"Bill, fuck Patriot, alright. You're doing your best, and that's all that matters, bro. I love you, man. I had that fool pick me up just so I could see my best friend. I missed you, man. I fucking hate that guy, come on now. Don't let that stupid shit get to you," Mike says, trying to cheer Bill up, but it's not working. Bill just continues puffing on the joint. Mike turns and sees October checking out Bill.

"Bro, October hella wants you. Go make a fucking move, dawg. Now's the chance to get with her," Mike says as Bill then turns around and locks eyes with October.

She smiles as she looks deeply into his eyes. Danny comes downstairs, and he picks up Lola. Lola giggles a bit as Danny then starts heading up the stairs, carrying her.

"You stole my dancing partner, you fucking asshole, Danny!" Girl yells as Danny makes it all the way up the stairs.

"Fuck off, we fucking! Stay downstairs, guys, this is gonna be some freaky, kinky, crazy sex!" Danny yells back from upstairs. His voice echoes throughout the cabin and throughout the woods.

Girl chugs the rest of her beer and sets the empty bottle on the small wooden table next to the boom box. She then drunkenly walks over to October.

"My dancing partner is gone, but you know how to dance way better, so you'll be dancing with me, bitch," Girl says, slurring her words and trying her best to remain still.

October laughs at her stupidity. She then sets her beer on the floor and stands up. Girl cheers as they dance around the living room together, drunk and alive. October starts to dance in front of Bill. She turns around and bends over in front of him, shaking her ass around for him. Girl sees this and decides to dance in front of the boys too. Girl dances wildly. She then turns to both boys and lifts up her sweater. Since she's not wearing a bra, she flashes and shows them her boobs.

October turns and sees this. Mike and Bill are blushing. They both just continue to stare at Girl as she takes off her sweater and throws it at Bill. She then continues to dance in front of them. October stares down Bill. Her eyes go from green to red as she continues to stare at him.

Bill is laughing, smoking, and now slapping Girl's ass. Girl is enjoying the attention. She turns and sits on Bill's lap. She takes the joint out of his mouth and smokes it, inhaling and exhaling the marijuana.

"Damn, Billy, you are just a fuckup, huh?" October asks. She stares at Girl while tears fall down her face. Bill grabs both of Girl's breasts and starts laughing.

"I'm getting lucky tonight!" Bill yells. He then takes the joint out of Girl's mouth and starts smoking the rest of it.

October looks at Bill, disgusted by his demeanor. "Fuck you, Bill! Fuck you! Fuck you too, Girl! You dumb fucking whore!" October screams and then storms out of the living room and into the kitchen. Bill pushes Girl off, and she falls onto the floor laughing. Bill then turns to Mike.

"I need to go outside and take a breather," Bill says as he starts to head toward the front door.

Mike stands up and follows. "I'll accompany you," he says as Bill opens the door, and they both head outside, shutting the door, never opening it again.

It's cold outside, and there's no sound other than the music coming from the inside. It's midnight, and the only light is the porch light. Mike and Bill walk away from the cabin but not too far from the porch light. Bill throws the roach on the ground and searches his pockets for another joint. He finds one and pulls it out. Mike hands Bill a lighter.

"I'm dumb as fuck. Yeah, a little bit drunk and really fucking high, but I'm just dumb in general, man," Bill says as he then lights up the joint and takes a hit.

"Well, yeah, you definitely fucked up with October, but I guess you can fuck Girl now. Lucky you. Ha-ha," Mike says.

"Girl? What kind of fucking name is that?" Bill asks as he hands the joint to Mike.

"Girlenza is her real name. She hates it because everyone always fucks up saying it and spelling it. I had her in drama and in history, bro. She's a total fucking flirt. Literally toys with every guy she meets, including Joint too," Mike says as he takes a hit and then passes the joint back to Bill.

"Hey, man, something feels off, like bad vibes. Earlier on our drive here, Danny's fucking passenger window just shatters randomly."

Mike looks at Bill, confused. "What do you mean randomly?" he asks.

Bill takes a hit and passes the joint back to Mike. They pass the joint back and forth until all the marijuana is smoked. Mike throws the roach on the ground and stomps on it with his right foot.

"It was some sound, some odd noise that shattered the window. It could've been a rock. Maybe I'm just tripping," Bill says, shaking.

"Alright, man, it's getting a bit cold outside. Let's head back, Bill." Mike turns around and starts walking toward the cabin's front door.

The quietness outside is interrupted by a loud tree branch cracking. Mike stops moving; he then turns back around to see Bill staring into the darkness of the woods. Another crack is heard—this time the sound is closer. Mike and Bill look at each other for a second.

"Hello?" Bill calls out.

Mike walks up to Bill, and they both start to look around into the darkness. A grunt is heard coming out of the woods. The grunt is distorted; it echoes and rings in Mike's and Bill's ears.

"What the actual fuck!" Bill says as he then walks into the darkness. He looks around a bit and then turns back looking at Mike.

A shadow now hovers above Bill. Mike looks up, and his jaw drops.

"Mike, why are you looking at me like that? What the fuck, bro?" Bill asks.

Another tree branch cracks behind Bill. Mike looks at Bill with fear in his eyes. Bill turns around and sees a rusty machete swinging at him, slicing his neck. Bill doesn't feel anything. Blood starts to pour out of his neck as he falls to the ground, with his head rolling off and hitting Mike's feet. Mike looks down at his best friend's head. Bill's eyes are still open, and they stare deeply into Mike's eyes.

"Fuck! Fuck! *Fuck*! Holy fucking shit! Shit, fuck, fuck, fucking shitty fuck! What the fuck!" Mike yells.

He looks up at the murderer in front of him. It's a creature of some sort, with gray wrappings around its face. Some burnt skin shows, and the left eye is uncovered and bright red. The creature is very tall and bulky, and it wears a black robe with chain mail. The creature's feet are covered by black boots, and its hands are both burnt and disfigured, with some bones showing. Mike takes a big step backward, shaking and sweating. The creature takes a big step forward and crushes Bill's head with its right foot.

Blood and brain pieces splatter onto Mike, who then swings his left fist at the creature. Since the machete is in the creature's right hand, the creature uses its left hand to grab Mike's fist. The creature crushes Mike's hand, breaking every bone. Mike screams as the creature holds onto his hand. The machete then swings down, and it slices off Mike's left arm. Mike falls to the ground, free from the creature's grasping hand. He quickly picks himself back up and makes a run toward the cabin's front door. Blood is pouring out of Mike, hitting the grass, coloring it.

Mike makes it halfway and trips. He struggles to get up this time. The music inside the cabin becomes louder and louder. Mike gets up, but it's too late. The machete swings again, and it cuts off Mike's other arm. Mike falls onto his back. Looking up, he sees the creature in front of him. The creature grabs Mike by the neck with its left disfigured hand. The creature looks into Mike's crying fearful eyes and hisses loudly. The wrapping around the creature's mouth unfolds, showing and exposing a mouth with no lips, just teeth. Its teeth are sharp and triangular like a shark's tooth.

"You have awakened me from my slumber ten thousand years too early. And for that you and all your friends will die tonight," the creature says, speaking to Mike with its deep and distorted voice.

"Someone fucking help me!" Mike screams from the top of his lungs, crackling his voice.

The music inside the cabin is so loud no one hears his cries or his screams. Mike is then lifted up and thrown into the cabin's front door. The door busts down and breaks easily. Girl jumps up off the couch frantically. She screams as she sees that Mike is missing both of his arms. The wood from the door has cut Mike up, putting splinters into his face. Girl screams again as the creature enters the cabin, presenting itself in front of her.

"What the fuck is that thing! What the fuck is happening! Help! Danny, Bill, someone fucking help me!" Girl yells.

She looks at the creature up and down and then stares at the rusty, bloody machete. The machete is so rusty its orange appears dull. Girl moves to the right corner by the rocking chair, shaking and still staring at the machete. She freezes and waits for the creature's next move.

"You have awakened me from my slumber ten thousand years too early. And for that you and all your friends will die tonight," the creature says, looking deeply into Girl's eyes.

She starts to cry as the creature walks up to Mike.

Mike looks at Girl. "*Run*! Get the fuck outta here!" Mike yells.

Those were his last words. The machete swings down, and it slices Mike's head in half. The creature leaves the machete and then turns to Girl. The creature walks toward her and then stops at the fireplace.

The creature puts its hands by the fire and feels its warmth. Girl, shaking and crying, watches the creature's every move. The creature looks up and sees the shotgun.

"Please, just fucking go away please. I have a bright future ahead of me. Please let me go. Let me leave," Girl says, crying loudly.

The creature grabs the shotgun and points it at her.

"It's not loaded, you ugly fuck!" Girl yells.

The shotgun fires, exploding Girl's beautiful face, destroying her makeup. Blood and parts of her brain splatter onto the wall as her deceased body slides to the ground. The creature aims the shotgun at the boom box and shoots it. The boom box is destroyed, ending the music, with the gun sound and Girl's last scream echoing in every room in the cabin.

CHAPTER 3

A HERO'S SACRIFICE

Girl's scream, the music cutting off, and the sound of a shotgun make Patriot, October, and Joint jump from the stools of the kitchen bar. All three of them look at each other, confused and worried.

"You fucking heard that right?" Patriot asks. October starts to shake.

"I'm not just on hella drugs. We all heard that, right?" Patriot asks again.

Joint, panicked, hops over the bar and knocks down a few shot glasses and beer bottles. They break instantly when they hit the floor. The sound of the glass shattering echoes in the kitchen. October looks at Patriot, scared and unknowing of what to do next. Footsteps are now heard coming toward them.

"October, go hide in the pantry and don't come out until I say so!" Patriot yells.

She instantly follows his command and runs to the pantry. She quickly opens the door and shuts it then throws herself onto the floor and hides underneath a long shelf that's full of canned goods.

Patriot looks ahead and sees a dark shadow standing a few feet from him. The creature takes a step forward and exposes itself to Patriot. The creature is empty-handed, and its red eye just stares down Patriot. Patriot looks back at the bar; he sees one full shot glass. He quickly takes it, drinks it, and then throws the shot glass at the creature.

The shot glass smashes as it hits the creature's face, cutting some of its wrappings and exposing more of its gray, burnt skin. The creature starts to walk slowly toward Patriot. Joint looks up quickly and sees the creature too. He quickly ducks down and lays flat on the floor, trying to hide himself.

"You have awakened me from my slumber ten thousand years too early. And for that you and all your friends will die tonight," the creature says, speaking directly to Patriot with its distorted voice echoing.

"Yeah, ain't that so! You know what, fucker? You gonna have to take us all on, motherfucker! We will not go down dead without a fucking fight, bitch!" Patriot yells as he drunkenly charges at the creature with closed fists.

The creature quickly punches Patriot in the face with a right hook that instantly breaks his nose and knocks him to the ground. Blood starts to pour out of Patriot's nose and mouth. He gets up, but everything is dizzy and red. Another punch hits the left side of Patriot's face, which also knocks a few teeth out in front. Patriot is then grabbed and slammed onto the floor. Patriot, now angered and in rage mode, gets up quickly and swings at the creature with both fists. The creature dodges him and then punches him in the face with another right hook.

Patriot falls to the floor, crying and unable to move. The creature takes off Patriot's hat and throws it at the bar. The hat lands on Joint, who then peeks out from the left side behind the bar. He watches as the creature grabs Patriot's hair with both hands and slams his face on the floor. The creature repeatedly slams Patriot's face on the floor until the kitchen tiles are covered in his blood. Patriot doesn't scream, doesn't call for help, and doesn't even try to fight back. He takes it like a champion or like someone who has earned this punishment. After three more floor-face slams, the creature stops.

Joint, who's still peeking out from the left side from behind the bar, watches as the creature leaves the kitchen. Joint's eyes then turn to Patriot who is motionless. Joint waits five minutes and then rushes over toward Patriot. He flips Patriot over and cries as he sees the horror the creature has done to him. Patriot's face is completely covered in blood; his nose is broken, his lips are fat with blood leaking out, and he's missing all his front teeth.

"I'm fucking sorry, Patriot. You dumb crazy motherfucker you. I knew something bad happened as soon as the music got cut off. You fucking hero," Joint says as he stares at Patriot, hoping he would move.

"Why the fuck did you try to fight that thing?" Joint asks.

October opens the pantry door, and the first thing she sees is Patriot's face. She cries as the image is unforgettable and implanted into her brain.

"Is Patriot dead?" October asks Joint. She walks over and picks up Patriot's hand.

"Look at him, he's fucking dead. A beating like that would kill anyone. Look, we need to leave and go find the others if they're alive. After that, we barricade and hide out for a bit until morning. I don't know. I'm sorry, I'm so fucking high," Joint says, trying to calm the situation.

Joint grabs October's hand, and they both leave the kitchen, now entering the living room. The living room is empty with no life. The dead bodies of Mike and Girl are seen by October and Joint.

"No! They Are All Dead!" October screams.

She lets go of Joint's hand and then walks up and stares at Girl's corpse. Joint looks at Mike and pulls the machete out of his head with his right hand. Mike's head splits completely in two, with the right side of his face falling and splattering on the floor.

"Mike was a good kid. Young and stupid, but he had lots of great things coming his way. His life was taken away too soon and unfairly. I'm gonna fucking kill whoever is responsible for these murders. These were my fucking friends," Joint says out loud, crying as he then turns and looks at Girl's body.

"I never got the chance to tell her. To tell her how I really felt. I loved Girl. I just let her do her thing. Maybe in another dimension, she might have loved me too," Joint says, wiping the tears off his face.

October looks at him. "You loved her?" she asks.

"I always have. I just was too pussy to make a fucking move. I thought tonight we would hopefully make up. That's not gonna happen now. She's fucking dead, headless," Joint says as he walks over to the rocking chair and takes a seat.

October puts her arm on his shoulder. Joint just sits there silently, faced down looking at the machete.

"Joint, I'm gonna go upstairs and check to see who's all left. If something happens, I will yell and scream for you. I need you to be strong and ready. You still have me, Joint, and I've always liked you. I'm sorry about Girl," October says as she then quickly dashes off and runs upstairs bravely.

"I'll just stay here and wait. I will fucking kill this monster. I will fucking avenge them all," Joint quietly says, speaking to himself. He looks up and starts to look around the living room, inspecting the damage. His eyes land on Mike's body. Joint stares at the floor, looking at a piece of Mike's face. Joint pukes all over himself and then falls to the floor. He looks back at Mike's face and then looks upward at the missing front door. A white dash blinds him for a second. Joint rubs his eyes and sees an all-white creature in front of him slither away into the darkness of the night.

October, upstairs, hears a noise coming from one of the bedrooms. She listens carefully and hears the noise coming from the last room on the right side. She walks slowly toward the room to investigate. She jumps when she hears the sounds of two people. She tries to open the door, but it's locked. She then puts her ear on the door and hears moaning coming from a man and a woman. October's face turns red. She then angrily kicks open the door and sees Lola naked on top of Danny. They are having sex loudly on the bed.

Danny smiles as he stares at October. Lola covers her breasts and gives October a "what the fuck" type of look. October stares at them both, angered.

"Patriot, Girl, and Mike are fucking dead! Fucking dead! You guys are just upstairs fucking the whole time while everyone's fucking dying!" October yells.

Lola gets off of Danny and rushes to put her clothes back on. Danny just lies there, naked and confused.

"What's going on?" he asks October.

"Some fucking freak came in uninvitedly and killed our friends! Patriot is in the kitchen with his face smashed in, Mike's missing both of his arms, and Girl's head is all over the fucking wall! Danny, we need to fucking move!" October yells again.

Danny quickly gets up, and October blushes as she stares at all his nakedness. Danny quickly puts his clothes back on as October just watches.

"Danny, umm, nice dick by the way. Lola, he's fucking packing, that's a big dick," October says, smiling as she left the room.

Danny grabs Lola's hand, and they follow October out of the room and down the stairs. Danny and Lola see the dead bodies of Mike and Girl. Danny looks down at the floor and stares at a piece of Mike's face looking into his eye. He then looks up and turns around to see Joint sitting in the rocking chair covered in vomit. Danny lets go of Lola's hand and walks toward Joint. He almost trips on something, and when he looks down, he sees the double-barrel shotgun. He picks it up and gives it to October.

"Hold this for a second," Danny demands, and she follows his command, grabbing the shotgun.

"Joint, are you okay?" Danny asks him.

"Don't go into the kitchen. You wouldn't want to see your best friend dead as fuck. I think Bill is dead too," Joint says with an angry tone.

Danny looks away from Joint and stares at the destroyed front door. Without thinking, he walks outside. Lola tries to stop him, but Danny pushes her away.

"Babe? Babe, what the fuck are you doing?" Lola asks as she follows Danny outside.

Danny ignores her and walks a little and then stops. He looks at one of Mike's missing arms and then follows a blood trail with his eyes until they land on Bill's deceased body.

"Bill? That can't be Bill," Danny says, staring at the varsity jacket. He then looks down and sees his brother's smashed head. Danny starts to cry uncontrollably.

Lola looks at Bill and then pukes.

"Babe! Get the fuck back inside! *Now*!" Danny yells, scaring Lola off.

She sprints back inside the cabin while Danny walks over and picks up Bill's body. He then starts to walk back toward the cabin, carrying Bill.

"I failed you, my little brother. My baby brother. My only family left. I failed you, Bill, I fucking failed you," Danny says out loud, hoping that Bill's spirit heard. "I'm sorry, my brother," he says as he enters the cabin.

October and Joint stare at Bill, getting the closure, solving the mystery of what happened to Bill. October starts to cry.

"What the fuck do we do, Danny?" Joint asks him.

Danny just looks at Joint, and they play the staring contest while October starts to cry louder.

October throws the shotgun on the couch and then drops to the floor.

"I fucking loved that asshole! Fuck you, Bill! Fuck you!" October cries out. She then sits on the floor with both hands covering her face. Some of her tears hit the floor like raindrops. The power suddenly goes out, making the cabin darker inside.

"Let's move the couch and block the entrance first. After that, we will pile the dead bodies on top of the couch to create more of a barrier. After that, barricade everything else, all windows too," Danny says, looking at everyone.

"We need to call the police, babe!" Lola says, yelling at Danny, scared and shaking.

"Police?" Danny asks with a confused look. "No cellular service out in these woods, dipshit! No fucking phone line, no fucking nothing!" Danny yells.

"Do what the fuck I say, and maybe we will all get outta this alive!" he yells again, this time toward everyone.

"We are all gonna die," October says quietly.

Danny drops Bill's body on the couch, grabs the shotgun, and then starts to push the couch toward the entrance. Joint gets off the rocking chair and helps. They get the job done quickly and easily. Joint and Danny then move the two dead bodies on top of the couch to barricade the front more.

"What about the cars? Do you have the keys, Danny?" October asks.

"Well, Patriot's car is out of gas. He ran out right when we pulled up. We were gonna rob you for some after vacation, Danny," Joint says, laughing.

"I have the keys, but I don't think it's safe to go back outside right now. We should wait to make our escape. We just don't know what the fuck we are dealing with," Danny says, speaking to everyone.

"How about you throw me your keys and I'll go start the car up?" says October, being demanding.

"Alright, fuck it! Wanna go outside and be a fucking hero? Make a fucking hero's sacrifice! Do it!" Danny yells as he walks over and gets in October's face. He then sets the shotgun on the floor next to her.

"Danny, I'm scared, okay? I just want to get us all out of here. We will all die waiting. This fucking thing will kill us all. Patriot, Mike, Girl, and Bill are fucking dead. Seems like they were killed off instantly. Hand me the keys, please. I'll get us all out of here, Danny. It'll be quick," October says, looking up at Danny crying.

Danny digs in his left pocket and pulls out his car key. October snatches it quickly out of his hand.

"Please just don't die on us. Please be safe." October hugs Danny.

Joint moves the couch back, far enough for October to squeeze her tiny body through. She makes it through and runs toward the cars. As she approaches Danny's Ford, she notices that the wheels have all been slashed.

"Fuck it. I still have to try," October quietly says to herself.

She walks over to the driver's side and unlocks the door using the key. She opens the door, but before she can get in, the door is kicked, making it slam against her face. Her glasses fall to the ground, shattering into little pieces. Blood pours down her face as she touches upward and feels that her head has been split open. October is suddenly grabbed and thrown on to the ground. She struggles to get back up, and when she does, she's kicked back down. A black boot then stomps her out until she's lifeless. A hero's sacrifice.

CHAPTER 4

ALIVE AIN'T WELL

Danny and Joint are sticking their heads above the couch, looking around outside.

"Danny, October isn't back. She didn't start the car up," Joint says, worried.

"I know. She's fucking dead. I have a feeling that this fucker sabotaged my car. I think it was a trap, and October fell for it and paid the price with her life. I promise you, Joint, no one else will die tonight. We gotta figure something else out," Danny says silently to Joint.

Danny and Joint then walk back over toward Lola who's sitting in the rocking chair. She's rocking the chair back and forth, making the wood floors creak.

"Alright, new plan. Babe, listen up," Danny says, looking deeply into his fiancée's eyes.

"October, she's dead, right?" Lola asks. She looks away from Danny and stares at the floor. She starts to cry.

"Yes, she's fucking dead, okay? The new plan right now is to find some weapons and supplies. After that we wait a little bit and then make a run for it. If we don't do something soon or if we leave now, we will all end up like her," Danny says as he then storms off into the kitchen, angered and frustrated.

"My two friends are dead. I'm just scared that I'll be next," Lola says, looking up to Joint.

"My friends are dead too, and I know I won't make it out alive tonight. I'll be murdered at midnight," Joint says as Lola just stares at him listening.

"Look, just stay here, okay? Yell if something happens. I'm going to go see what Danny's up to. He's right though. Just understand that, Lola," Joint says, handing the rusty machete to Lola.

She slowly grabs it and watches Joint leave the living room. As Joint enters the kitchen, the first thing he notices is a missing body. Patriot's dead body is missing, only a blood spill remains on the tiles. Joint turns to the bar and sees Patriot sitting on a stool to the far left, hiding in a dark shadow as if he wanted to be hidden away. Danny is seen just standing there looking at Patriot.

Patriot picks up a bottle of rum from the counter and raises it up. He chugs the drink quickly and throws the bottle on the floor, watching it shatter into pieces.

"Where…is…October?" Patriot asks, trying to talk. He stands up and kicks the barstool down and then moves toward his two friends.

"Patriot, how the fuck are you alive? I saw that thing fuck you up badly," Joint asks, staring at his friend's bloodstained face.

Patriot moves closer. "I was unconscious. I can't talk. My tongue is cut, I only have six teeth. I count," Patriot says, trying to talk. Every time he opens his mouth, blood pours and spits out. Patriot starts to cry. Danny walks over and gives him a hug.

"Don't talk, man. Save your strength for action. I'm very happy you made it, Patriot. Girl, Mike, Bill, and October are all dead. They are fucking dead, man. Dead," Danny says, still hugging Patriot as they both cry together. Joint, watching, smiles.

"Alive ain't well," Joint says. He walks over to the kitchen and takes off his shirt and throws it in the sink. He then starts to open a couple of drawers by the sink, hoping he will find a weapon. In the last drawer, he finds a large kitchen knife and grabs it.

CHAPTER 5

TABLE TALK

The four remaining survivors are in the kitchen, sitting in the chairs that surround the long kitchen table. Joint is sitting next to Patriot while Lola and Danny are sitting next to each other across from them. Supplies and weapons are scattered all over the table, ungrouped and uncounted.

"Alright, we got fifteen water bottles, two bags of potato chips, one large uncooked pizza, two bags of weed, which both look about one ounce each, two bottles of scotch, two bottles of vodka, a bottle of Fireball, a set of matches, a working shotgun with no shells, a dull-ass machete, and two kitchen knives," Danny says out loud, looking at each item on the table.

Joint slides the machete toward himself while Danny just watches. Lola then suddenly starts to cry.

"Don't forget the canned pineapple and peaches in the pantry," Joint says, speaking directly to Danny.

Danny turns and hugs Lola. She kisses Danny on the lips and stops crying.

"Fuck the peaches. We all need to pick a weapon and then find a trash bag or something to carry the rest of this shit," Danny says.

Patriot looks at Danny, wanting to say something ridiculous and outrageous. Danny looks back at his friend with fear in his eyes.

"I call dibs on the machete. I found it first," Joint says as he picks up the machete and twirls it around.

"You want the weapon that beheaded my brother?" Danny asks as he stares at Joint with hatred.

"It also split Mike's head in fucking half and chopped off both of his arms. Mike suffered, your brother didn't. Yes, I want the machete, I found it first," Joint answers.

"No, Joint, you get the kitchen knife. I'm gonna use that machete and chop that fucker into bits and fucking pieces," Danny says, almost raising his voice.

Joint angrily gets up and points the machete at Danny. Patriot then starts to laugh wildly.

"Do you understand me? Do you understand, Joint?" Danny asks him.

Joint drops the machete on the table. A couple of water bottles fall and roll off the table.

"You stupid high fuck. Sit down before I kick your fucking ass for being fucking stupid," Danny demands.

Joint sits back down quickly. "Danny, I'm sorry, man. I love you. I'm just losing it, man," Joint says as he then grabs the bottle of Fireball and starts to drink it. He chugs the entire bottle as everyone else around the table watches in amazement.

"Fuck it. Keep it. Just promise me that you'll do exactly what I have intended on doing with it. Fucking promise me, Joint," Danny says, tearing up a little. He slams his right fist on the table. A couple more water bottles fall and roll off the table, hitting the kitchen tiles with a splash.

"Danny, I'm fucking sorry, okay? It's only us right now! Grab your girl and go fuck her for the last time! Then shut the fuck up and let's figure out some fucking plan or something fuck!" Joint yells, apologetically and seriously.

"I just don't want this killer zombie fuck to come back. Honestly, let's go," Joint says.

Lola and Danny both look at him with confusion. Patriot starts to shake as he now remembers more of his beatdown.

"A zombie?" Lola asks.

"I don't know what the fuck I saw. But it's not human. A mummy or some creature of the night. Fuck it. From here on out, it's called the creature of the night," Joint says, trying to be informative.

Lola, Danny, and Patriot stare Joint down. Joint looks around at all the eyes looking at him.

"I'm the only one who saw it. Well, Patriot did too, but I speak for him. This creature of the night is strong, okay? Patriot was the strongest in the group, and he got fucked the fuck up by that thing. We need to find shotgun shells so we can blow this fucker's head off or chop it off with the weapons we got," Joint says, breathing heavily and sweating a little. He looks around at the items on the table and grabs a bottle of vodka.

Danny, Lola, and Patriot watch as Joint chugs the bottle halfway. He quickly launches off his chair to the left and starts to puke all over the kitchen tiles.

Patriot starts to laugh. As he smiles, blood pours out of his mouth, alarming Danny who notices.

"Joint, you fucking idiot," Lola says, laughing and smiling at Joint's stupidity.

Patriot stands up and pushes in his chair. He grabs the shotgun, steps over some puke, and starts to walk toward the living room.

"Patriot? What are you doing, man?" Danny asks quickly before Patriot left the kitchen.

Patriot turns and smiles with more blood leaking out of his mouth. He starts to wave the shotgun side to side.

"I find…shotshells," Patriot says, trying his best to speak to his best friend. Patriot then turns back around and leaves the kitchen.

Upon entering the living room, a white figure dashes from outside the couch barricade. Patriot notices and decides to walk toward the couch, staring at the bodies of Mike, Bill, and Girl which lay on top of it. He stops halfway as something dashes out in front of him again, this time coming from the left. Patriot continues to stare into the darkness outside the cabin. The white figure slowly moves to the right, presenting itself to Patriot. He stares at this average-sized full white creature.

The creature has four black circular eyes, no mouth, and four small white tentacles which seemed to have emerged from its sides. The creature is all white with silky smooth skin. Patriot plays the staring contest with it until he loses. The creature is now gone as if it had vanished or if it was some illusion, something in Patriot's mind. Patriot quickly turns away and runs upstairs, trying to figure out what he just saw.

CHAPTER 6

THE ALIEN

The living room is cold; the fire is out. Danny, who's sitting by the fireplace with Lola, burns the wood using a match. The fire starts up again, but the room is still cold. Joint is sitting on the rocking chair watching as the couple tries to get warm together.

"Where's Patriot?" Joint asks aloud.

"I assume he's upstairs still looking for shotgun shells or something," Danny says as he grabs Lola and pulls her closer toward himself. Lola puts her arms around Danny, and they cuddle up by the fire. Joint starts to laugh.

"I'm gonna die alone. I have no one," Joint says with tears falling down his face.

Danny and Lola both look at him. "You have us. No one else is dying tonight. We will not be murdered at midnight. We will live to tell our tale. Once Patriot finds some shells for that shotgun, it's fucking hunting season for this zombie fucker," Lola says, trying to cheer up and give some hope to Joint who's losing it mentally.

"Well, what the fuck do we do while we wait?" Joint asks.

"I remember when I was in college and I always caught Bill smoking out by the dumpster. The apartment we lived in was small and ghetto. I remember when we almost got kicked out because the landlord caught Joint and Bill smoking out of a big-ass bong. I remember yelling at you two and calling Bill a dumb stupid motherfucker. I hope I wasn't too hard on my brother. I only wanted the best for him. Shit, I even thought this little vacation up here would fix our relationship. It's too late for that now. I just wish I could go back to those good old days. Back when we were all young and alive. Young and stupid. I miss that. I miss my brother," Danny says, fake laughing and then crying.

Lola hugs him and then kisses his lips. Danny and Lola look into each other's eyes, trying to find comfort.

"I remember when I first fell in love with you, Danny. I also remember Girl telling me to not even go for it. I'm so lucky to have you in my life even though we are stuck in this hell right now. My feelings for you don't change. I know you'll protect us, babe," Lola says, staring deeply into Danny's eyes. She kisses his lips again and again. She then wipes away Danny's tears and kisses him again.

"I remember when I dated Girl, I said I love you on the seventh day. That's the day we broke up because she fucked some other guy. What's fucked is that I actually meant it. I love her, I always loved her. Now she's dead and gone. She's been taken from me," Joint says, staring at Lola and Danny.

Lola and Danny stop kissing, and they look up at Joint.

"I remember Patriot always fucking with me. He always talks this guy. He runs his fucking mouth like a fool. Now he doesn't speak, and if he does, blood pours out. I remember playing video games with my two best friends. Now Mike and Bill are both fucking dead. I remember first meeting October. She was alone at lunch, and I intruded because I was also alone that day and didn't want to be. We talked, and she soon became one of my best friends. Now she's gone and dead. All her sweetness and joy went with her too. We lost our friends. No, we lost our family," Joint says in a depressed tone. Right in front of Joint's feet is a small glass bong. He picks it up and pulls out a lighter from his right pocket and starts to smoke out of the bong.

"Now look at us. Hurt, scared, and unknowing of what to do next," Lola says, watching as Joint clears the bong and coughs loudly.

"Danny, you're like a brother to me. A big brother. I'm sorry about Bill. He was a brother to me too. Bill was my first ever friend, and I'll miss him. In fact, I hope I die tonight so I can be with him. I wanna be with my friend," Joint says emotionally as he looks at Danny.

Danny stares back at him and feels all his numbness. Joint is done trying and doesn't care.

"Bill wouldn't want that. So try and live for him and for them. What fucking sucks is that if we do make it out of this, we won't be able to have open caskets for Bill, Mike, and Girl. They all don't have heads. I don't know about October, and to be honest, if she's dead, I don't want to see her corpse. Seeing Bill's headless body has already destroyed me as a person. That's my little fucking brother. He was only fucking twenty-three," Danny says, speaking to Joint with tears falling down his face.

Danny stands up and walks toward the couch barrier. He hovers above the couch, staring down at the dead bodies of Mike, Bill, and Girl. Danny looks at Bill, and suddenly, a swoosh coming from outside makes Bill's arm twitch and move. Danny's eyes widen as his brother's hand twitches, with his fingers moving. Danny starts to sweat as Lola and Joint then stand up and walk toward the couch. They try to speak, but everything around Danny is muted; he can't hear anything, he's too focused on his brother's hand. Joint suddenly drops the bong he was holding, and it breaks instantly as it hits the floor.

"It's okay, Danny. I can take you with me if you want." Bill's voice echoes in the living room, ringing and ringing in Danny's ears.

Tears pour out of Danny's eyes like rain. Thunder strikes in his eyes, and the sweat drops from his face, hitting the floor with a bang, like lightning. Danny freezes, and he doesn't know why. He tries to move, but he can't. He slowly looks up away from the hand, and standing in front of the doorway towering over the couch is the white creature Patriot saw and said nothing about. Patriot thought it was some illusion, but it's not; it's real. The creature and Danny look deeply into each other's eyes, so deep that they can both see their own reflections.

"That's the thing that killed my brother, right Joint?" Danny quietly asks as he continues to stare down the white creature.

Joint and Lola back up a little bit, staring down the creature. Lola quickly turns around and runs into the kitchen.

"I'm getting the machete!" she yells as she disappears into the kitchen.

"Danny! I don't know what the fuck that thing is! That's not what the fuck I saw! Something different killed Bill and the others! What the actual fuck!" Joint yells.

The creature's four black eyes all blink, scaring Joint a little bit, causing him to jump backward. Danny takes a big step backward and grabs Joint.

"Dude, it's just fucking looking at us. What the fuck," Danny says quietly to Joint.

"Do we attack it?" Joint asks as they both continue to stare down the creature.

The creature's four black eyes blink again. Danny and Joint watch as the creature slowly moves to the left and disappears into the darkness.

"What the fuck is that thing?" Danny asks.

"It's a fucking alien. No way something like that could ever exist on Earth. That white with four black circular eyes? Yeah, that's a motherfucking alien," Joint says, speaking fast.

Danny and Joint continue to stare out into the darkness, waiting for something to happen.

CHAPTER 7

THE PLAN

Patriot runs down the stairs in excitement. Danny and Joint meet him by the fireplace. Patriot smiles at them both and then holds out his left hand, showing the two friends two shotgun shells. Danny and Joint smile and jump in excitement. Patriot holds out the shotgun for either Danny or Joint to take.

"Good fucking job, man!" Joint yells.

"Where did you find them?" Danny asks.

"Master bedroom. In safe. In closet. Safe open," Patriot says, trying to talk.

Lola walks up to the group and holds out a machete and a large kitchen knife. Joint grabs the machete, the rusty machete that decapitated Bill and the weapon that also cut off Mike's arms. The weapon that killed both of his best friends. Joint remembers this weapon and also remembers his promise to Danny.

"Keep the shotgun, Patriot. I already promised Danny that I'd use this rusty-ass machete to slice up the creature of the night. The demon zombie fuck that killed our friends," Joint says. He then turns his back on the group and walks toward the couch barrier.

"I got a plan, and since Patriot found two shells, this plan will work out perfectly. I'll call out and find this creature of the night. I will then lure the creature inside, and that's when Patriot will shoot the fucker in the face. After it falls and dies, we all run outside. Either we find my car key from October's corpse or we fucking run straight into the woods. As long as we continue going straight, we will eventually find a road. We stay as a group, and we watch out for that alien thing stalking us," Danny says, speaking to the group, looking at each person separately. Danny turns around and looks at Joint, who's now wearing Bill's varsity jacket.

"A-alien?" Patriot asks.

Danny turns back around, looks at Patriot, and laughs. "Yeah, a fucking alien. All white with four black eyes," Danny says informatively.

Joint walks back over to the group, looking very angry. "What if you lure this fucking alien over here instead, Danny?" Joint asks, speaking in a very serious tone.

"Same plan, man. Guide the fucker inside and Patriot shoots it. Boom dead. Then we fucking run and live. Patriot, you have two chances. You fuck up, we all die," Danny says, answering Joint and then speaking directly toward Patriot.

Patriot nods as he understands his responsibilities with the double-barrel shotgun. Joint walks up and stands next to Danny, facing his right side.

"I kill the fucking monsters. I want revenge, Danny. I'm ready to kill," says Joint as he then gets in Danny's face.

Danny holds out his left hand and stares at the kitchen knife he's holding. "I'm pretty sure we can't kill these monsters with a kitchen knife and a rusty-ass machete," Danny says, speaking to Joint directly.

Joint grabs the kitchen knife from Danny's left hand and walks back toward the couch barrier. He looks down at the two weapons he's holding and laughs.

"What do I do?" Lola asks silently.

Danny turns to his right and stares at Lola. He smiles and looks at her while moving his head up and down.

"What are you doing, babe?" Lola asks Danny with a puzzled look on her face.

"I just want to stare at all of you and remember all of your beauty. Just in case something does happen, and if so…we got you plan fucking B," Danny says, speaking to his fiancée, being as serious as he can be.

"What's plan fucking B? Why me?" Lola asks.

Danny just continues to stare at her.

"Is it me running into the woods alone?" Lola asks, knowing that she had answered her own question.

"I love you. Lola, even if you run out there alone, I'll find you. If I'm hurt, dying, and or missing my fucking arms, I'll find you, my love. Don't be afraid, find help and live," Danny says, looking into Lola's eyes like it was going to be for the last time ever.

"DANNY, No!" Lola yells. "I can't lose you, babe! Patriot you better not fucking miss!" she yells at the two of them.

Patriot reloads the empty shotgun with the two shells he found. He puts the shotgun in his right hand and then uses his left hand to dig in his left pocket. He laughs as he pulls out a small baggie half full of crushed cocaine. He opens the bag and dumps all the cocaine on his face. He then shakes his head fast, wipes away the rest off his face using his left hand, and then proceeds upstairs, waiting on the fourth step to attack.

"Well, alright then. Ha-ha," Danny says, laughing.

Lola rushes over and gives Danny a hug. Danny hugs her back and then kisses her all over. He kisses her lips, her cheeks, her forehead, and then her neck. He leaves a huge hickey on the right side of Lola's neck, leaving a love bite she won't forget. Joint laughs as he watches the two lovers make out.

"I've waited long enough. Your deaths are key to making peace within the woods. My slumber here is key to keeping evil contained," the distorted voice said, echoing in the living room.

Danny, Lola, and Joint all turn and see the creature of the night staring at them from behind the couch barrier. The creature of the night is somewhat hidden by the darkness outside.

"Awakening me ten thousand years too early, forcing me to kill so I can then earn back my sleep," the creature of the night says, with its distorted voice echoing in the living room again.

"LOLA! FUCKING RUN! FUCKING HIDE!" Danny yells as he pushes Lola toward the kitchen.

She looks at Danny with tears in her eyes and then runs into the kitchen crying. The creature of the night continues to stare at Danny and Joint from behind the couch barrier, being silent and immovable like a statue.

"Why are you doing this? Why did you kill my little brother?" Danny asks.

The creature ignores him and continues to stare.

"You Took My Brother From Me, You Fuck!" Danny says, yelling at the creature with pure anger and hate.

The creature of the night kicks the couch barrier, and it moves back far enough for entry. The dead bodies of Bill, Mike, and Girl all fall on the floor. The creature of the night then starts to walk slowly toward Joint and Danny. Joint runs right at the creature, swinging the rusty machete in his right hand. He swings the machete, cutting the creature of the night's face.

The gray wrappings on the creature's face fall off from being cut, exposing the creature's mutated, mutant, skeleton-like burnt face. Joint's eyes widen as his fear level rises and rises. The creature of the night has no nose, no ears, no lips, and no skin around its left eye, making the eyeball pop out a bit. Both red eyes stare deeply into Joint's eyes, staring deeply into his soul. Joint swings the machete again, but this time, the creature blocks its face with its left arm, causing the rusty and dull machete to break. Its pieces fly into the air and then hit the cabin's floor. Joint quickly uses the large kitchen knife he has in his left hand and stabs the creature of the night in the forehead. Joint leaves the knife in the creature's head and backs up a little bit. Danny and Joint are shocked that the creature didn't fall down dead. The creature slowly pulls out the kitchen knife with its disfigured, bony, and bloody right hand.

"Ohh, fuck me," Joint says as he looks at the creature with fear.

The creature dashes forward and stabs Joint in the right side of his chest. Joint instantly cries as the knife penetrates his skin. The creature moves the knife upward and then digs the rest of the blade into Joint's skin until a small piece of the handle is shown. Joint coughs up lots of blood, which pours out of his mouth. He looks at the creature's eyes and then falls to his knees.

"Leave him alone! It's me you want!" Danny yells.

The creature of the night grabs Joint, lifts him up, and then throws him at the rocking chair, breaking it and also knocking him out. Danny starts to shake as the creature now walks slowly toward him. Danny starts to back up. He passes the stairs and looks up at Patriot and then quickly back at the creature. Patriot moves down a step quietly and sees the creature approaching. The fire in the fireplace goes out as the creature of the night passes, making the living room cold instantly. The creature is about to pass the stairs, but Patriot jumps down quickly and points the shotgun right at the creature's ugly zombielike face. Patriot pulls the trigger, and the shotgun fires.

The creature of the night's head explodes with black blood showering down on Patriot's face. The creature falls to the floor right in front of Patriot's feet, headless. The black blood that's all over Patriot's face starts to melt and burn like acid. The black blood starts to sizzle on his face, removing the skin, instantly showing the bone. He turns around, freaking out and panicking. Danny runs to his best friend, thinking that he could possibly help Patriot and save him. Patriot turns to Danny and points the shotgun at him. Danny sees that Patriot is trying to actually point the gun at himself, but he can't lift it up. Patriot pushes upward with both hands and then quickly fires the shotgun.

The shotgun goes off, and Danny's head explodes. His body falls to the floor while Patriot drops the shotgun and then falls to his knees. Joint wakes up due to the shotgun going off and pushes himself against the wall behind him, lying on the floor and looking up at Patriot. Patriot's face is completely gone, with only bone showing. He has no eyes, no hair, no skin, and no ears. Patriot falls face first, hits the cabin's floor, and crushes his skull into bits and dies. Joint watches as parts of Patriot's skull scatter toward his feet. Joint starts to cry.

"Patriot, you stupid, stupid, stupid fuck. Crazy all the way until the very fucking end," Joint says, crying loudly. He looks down at the floor, staring at the three dead bodies. He looks at Danny, Patriot, the shotgun lying next to Patriot, and then at the creature of the night.

"How did you two die?" Joint asks himself as he tries to get up but instantly falls back down, sliding against the wall. He looks down at his chest and sees that a knife is buried deep inside his right pec. Joint suddenly starts to gush out blood all over himself.

"It's okay, Joint. I can take you with me too." Bill's voice echoes and echoes in the living room and in Joint's ears. Joint looks across the room at Bill's headless corpse.

"I ain't dying yet, fucker. I still have some fight left in me. Maybe," says Joint as he then closes his eyes, slides to the right, and falls, lying completely on the floor on his back. Good memories of smoking weed, hanging out with Bill, and kissing Girl for the first time play as if his life was flashing like a movie inside his head.

Joint smiles.

CHAPTER 8

PLAN B

Lola enters the living room and screams. The first thing her eyes caught was Danny's body. Danny lays next to Patriot; they are both dead and headless. Lola starts to cry.

"*Danny!*" she yells, hoping that he would respond. She realizes that he wouldn't be able to since he's headless. Lola looks around the living room until her eyes finally stop and land on Joint.

"They are all dead… Oh, fuck. I'm all alone now," Lola says, crying.

Suddenly, Joint moves. He lifts up his right arm and waves. "I'm not dead yet. But dying, yes, I can definitely feel that. Death is coming," Joint says, laughing and then coughing.

Lola rushes over to him. She grabs his torso with both hands and then pushes him up against the wall that was behind him.

"Lola, you need to run. Patriot's car is out of gas, and Danny's car key is with October. Just run into the woods like Danny said. There will be a road or street up ahead. Find help and live," Joint says, crying as he stares at Lola. More blood gushes out of his mouth and colors the varsity jacket he's wearing completely red.

Lola looks down at his chest and sees that the kitchen knife has been buried deep inside his right chest pec. "I can try to pull it out, and after that, we can both leave together. I need you right now. I can't go alone. There's that alien outside. Joint, I fucking need you," Lola says, crying and begging.

She watches as more blood gushes out of Joint's mouth. Joint laughs and then slowly looks around the living room, staring at all the carnage.

"I'm dying. Holy shit. This is what death feels like. It feels great," says Joint. He looks at Lola and stares deeply into her eyes.

"My real name is Jason. Danny named me Joint because I'm a stoner who loves smoking joints. I'd love to smoke one more before my passing," Joint says as he digs in his right pocket and pulls out a lighter.

Lola looks around the living room quickly and spots a joint lying on the small table where the boom box was before it was destroyed. She runs over, grabs it, and runs back to Joint quickly. She puts the joint in his mouth and also lights it up for him. Joint takes a puff and then smiles as he blows the smoke out of his nose. Lola puts the lighter in her right pocket and then crouches down in front of Joint, getting face-to-face with him.

"I'll go. But before I leave, what does your hand tattoo mean?" Lola asks as she looks down at Joint's left hand.

"Work hard, fight hard, and the fight between good and evil. The colorful rose signifies my trippy crazy life while the flaming skull getting punched by brass knuckles is work hard, fight hard, and the fight between good and evil. The skull is evil, and the brass knuckles are good. The brass represents us fighters," Joint says, answering Lola's question.

Lola smiles as Joint starts to smoke more of the weed. As Joint is smoking, he looks up and behind Lola. The creature of the night rises up, headless. The joint falls out of his mouth as he watches the creature taking off its chain mail armor. Lola turns around and stands up. The creature drops the chain mail armor on the floor to the right, next to Patriot's corpse. There's a small hole in the middle of the creature's black bloody robe. The creature opens up the hole with both hands and exposes a gigantic red eyeball in the middle of its chest.

The creature of the night's gigantic chest eye blinks, scaring Lola, causing her to jump back against the wall behind her. Joint slowly gets up, barely standing still and straight. The red eyeball just stares them both down.

"You need to run! Get the fuck outta here!" Joint yells.

Lola watches as Joint uses both hands to pull out the kitchen knife that was buried deep in his right chest pec. Joint, crying, turns over and looks at Lola.

"I'm already dead anyways. I deserve this. I was a horrible dumbass, smoking and being depressed. Now this ugly and bold man can now fucking sleep."

"You are a good man, Jason. Goodbye," Lola responds. She looks at Joint then turns her head and looks at the creature of the night and then finally looks down, staring at Danny's body.

"Goodbye, my love," Lola says, hoping that Danny heard. She then runs across the living room and dashes out of the cabin, disappearing into the darkness of the night.

The creature turns and watches as Lola exits the cabin; it then slowly turns back around to stare at Joint.

"That's right, you headless fuck! It's me you want!" Joint yells.

The creature starts to walk toward him. Joint gushes out blood, which covers the wall and floor on his left side.

"Alright, fuck it. But I ain't dying like no bitch. Plan B in action, and I guess I'm the distraction," Joint says, speaking to himself.

He watches as the creature gets closer toward him. He smiles and moves the kitchen knife from his right hand to his left hand. He extends out his left arm, pointing the knife at the creature. Joint looks at his hand tattoo.

"No gun, no ammo, no Danny, no friends, no weed, no girl, no coke, no drinks, no love, no way out, and finally no life because I knew I would die here in this fucking shitty shithole! Come get me, motherfucker! Try to kill me, Jason Michael, a.k.a. Joint!" Joint yells, charging at the creature with all the speed and strength that he has left.

The creature of the night blocks its chest eye with both hands, but the kitchen knife goes through both hands and reaches the large red eye. A white tentacle suddenly appears, and it slices off Joint's left hand. Joint cries out in pain as he watches his left hand fall to the floor in a pool of blood. He backs up, leaving the knife inside the creature's eye and watches as the tentacle impales the creature's eye and then slices upward and then downward, cutting the creature of the night in half, killing it for sure this time. The creature falls down dead sliced in two in front of Joint who looks down at his missing left hand.

"My fucking hand," Joint says as he looks up at the white alien in front of him.

Another tentacle emerges from the alien's right side. Joint watches as the alien slithers closer toward him. He looks away and starts to stare at the bodies of each of his friends that lay scattered across the living room. His eyes finally land on Girl's corpse. Joint just stares at her and doesn't move.

"I Love You!" he yells.

The alien's right tentacle impales Joint. He looks back at the alien and then down at his chest. Joint sees that the tentacle has impaled him through his stomach. He gushes blood out of his mouth, and his blood stains the tentacle more red.

"Fucking do it!" Joint yells, staring deeply at the alien and its four black circular eyes.

The tentacle moves, and it quickly exits Joint's body through his left side, cutting and gutting him open. Joint instantly falls to his knees with blood pouring and pouring out of his mouth and body. He looks down at the floor and sees his intestines dangling out of him, touching the floor. He looks back up at the alien and watches as the left tentacle slices toward his neck. The tentacle cuts off Joint's head. His head and body fall forward and splatter onto the cabin's floor. Joint's blood covers the white alien red.

The alien's two tentacles both carefully pick up Joint's head. The tentacles move, and they bring Joint's head closer toward the alien's face. The alien starts to glow orange as its face merges with Joint's head. Joint's closed dead eyes suddenly open and so does his mouth. The alien's face presses against Joint's face, and they combine together. The alien glows brightly as if a nuke had just gone off inside the cabin. The glow stops, and the alien has now transformed itself into Joint. The alien, or Joint, is naked, so he decides to take off the dead Joint's clothes, wearing it all proudly.

"This mission was easy. I just didn't know that Earth had other secrets and creatures," the alien disguised as Joint says. He smiles and exits the cabin in the most perfect disguise.

The real Joint lays on the cabin's floor headless, naked, and dead. The living room is filled with bodies, blood, guts, and brains all over the place. The living room is silent with just the bodies, no sound, no breathing, and no movement whatsoever.

CHAPTER 9

DISCOVERY AND DEATH

Lola, running into the dark woods, trips and falls to the ground. She quickly gets back up and looks down to see October lying in front of her. October's shirt is cut up with her left breast exposed, the right side of her face appears to be smashed in, and she looks like she has been ripped apart by some wild animals.

"October?" Lola says quietly.

October's chest moves, and her left eye opens. Lola looks down at her, surprised that she's actually still alive. October starts to breathe heavily and loudly, making Lola look around and panic a little bit.

"Shhhhh, shut the fuck up," says Lola. "October, I have to go. I have to leave you. Crawl and hide under Danny's car. I'll be coming back with help. Trust me,

I'll be back," Lola says as she looks at October and then turns, continuing her journey of running straight.

October watches as Lola disappears into the darkness of the woods. Lola runs for about ten minutes, running as fast as she can. Lola stops when she enters an area in the woods that's surrounded by trees that are gigantic, the biggest trees she has ever seen. The terrain in this area is rough as if an earthquake had happened. The ground is split up with dirt and rocks of all sizes making up most of the area. Lola looks around, confused. She walks straight and then looks down in front of her.

Lola finds broken tombstone pieces in front of an unburied wooden casket. She bends down and stares at the casket with curiosity. Lola extends out her arms and easily opens the casket. The casket is empty. Lola jumps when a tarantula is seen crawling around inside.

"Is this thing a fucking zombie?" Lola asks herself. "I don't know. But it did say that it woke up ten thousand years too early. The music was playing loudly, and my friends didn't cause this thing to wake up. That's a fucking fact."

Lola looks around some more and finds nothing. She continues to run straight ahead. As she is running, an orange light is seen ahead of her toward the left. As Lola gets closer, she notices that it's actually fire. The flames are huge, and they flair and flash brightly in the darkness. Lola stops running as she sees what has caused the fire: an unidentified flying object in the shape of a triangle is stuck in the ground. The UFO is gray, a bit destroyed, and small.

The front of the ship is smashed into the ground, buried, while the back of the ship is completely in flames. Lola stares at the UFO in amazement, admiring all of its glory and detail.

She starts to think, and then pieces everything together.

"Awakened me from my slumber. It wasn't us that woke up this creature of the night. It was this fucking alien visitor that did. It all makes sense now. The crash caused the creature to awaken early. It all makes fucking sense now," Lola says, quietly talking to herself.

"We didn't do anything but party and enjoy each other's company. In two weeks, I was going to get married. Oh, Danny, you, your brother, and your friends all died for nothing. We didn't cause this. We didn't fucking do anything wrong." Lola drops to her knees and starts to cry.

A noise interrupts her crying, a crack of a tree branch coming from an unknown direction. Lola looks around frantically, seeing nothing but darkness. Lola looks back at the UFO and sees a white figure standing behind the flames coming from the back of the ship. Another white alien with four black eyes and more slender. The alien stares at Lola with all fours eyes.

Lola screams at the alien, "Fuck you! Fuck you! You did this, not us! You fucking killed us!"

Lola stands up. She looks down at her feet and finds a decent-sized rock. She picks it up and throws it at the alien, hitting it in the face and knocking it down.

"Lola! *Stop*!" a voice yells out.

Lola watches as Joint appears out of the darkness in front of her. Joint walks over and stands next to the UFO.

"These aliens are friendly," Joint says, holding up both of his hands. He drops his hands to his sides and walks toward Lola.

Lola looks down and sees that Joint is missing his left-hand tattoo. "You are not my friend. Joint is dead," Lola says in an angered tone.

Joint laughs. "It's me, Jason. I'm alive. These aliens helped me," Joint says, trying to convince Lola.

"Jason doesn't call himself Jason. He's Joint. Also, you're missing the one thing that made him unique. His left-hand tattoo with the rose and brass knuckles hitting a skull. It means work hard and fight hard. For yourself, his friends, his family, and for all the other fighters in his life. If you don't have the tattoo, you're not him. I'm guessing you're some monster in his disguise," Lola says.

Joint looks down at his left hand and then laughs. "You humans are so fun. We came to this so-called Earth, or as we call it the blue and green planet, to study. Study everything like how you move, talk, eat, do things, and think. I just didn't know that this earth has other secrets like that thing that was killing your friends. I've only come in peace to study, but when I saw what was happening, I had to make a move, and I did," the Alien disguised as Joint says calmly and informatively.

"Are you going to kill me?" Lola asks. She looks around and sees that she's now surrounded by ten white aliens.

The aliens are slowly slithering toward her.

"You deserve to die. You have nothing left really. If Jason didn't engage in that fight with the creature of the night, I'd be wearing your face, Lola. Now I won't kill you, but maybe one of my comrades would love to wear your face and become you," the alien says, answering Lola and then smiling despicably.

"FUCK YOU!" Lola yells.

She looks around panicking and finds an opening straight ahead of her between two aliens. Lola sprints, running straight and barely dodging the two white aliens. As Lola runs, she turns her head back to see the two aliens following her from a distance. Lola quickly turns her head back forward and decides to run faster. The sound of a car driving can be heard up ahead. That sound excites Lola, and she decides to run even faster.

Lola sees blue and red lights in front of her. What she doesn't see is the hill that drops down before you can get to the road. Since it's so dark and the only light is the blue and red lights from the police car, Lola doesn't see the drop. Lola falls, tumbling down crying for help. A small tree sticks crookedly out of the ground below the drop. Lola's roll stops as she slams into the tree, impaling herself. In front of her is a police car which has pulled someone in a red truck over. Lola waves her hands around, but the darkness covers her up.

No one can see Lola. She tries to speak, tries to yell, and tries to move, but she can't. Warmth starts to hit her as she looks up to see the sunrise. The sunrise of a new day, a new beginning. But not for Lola as she looks forward to see the truck and the police car drive off toward the left away from her view. Lola smiles as blood starts to drip down from her lips. The tree breaks due to Lola's weight on it. She tumbles down more and then hits the street face first, cracking her neck and smashing in her entire face.

The two aliens look down the drop and stare at Lola's remains. Her head is split open, showing parts of her brain and skull. The two aliens look at each other and giggle. They both then turn around and slither back into the darkness of the woods, disappearing.

CHAPTER 10

THE ENDING

The sun shines brightly, making the cabin's old deteriorating wood more glamorous to the eye. Inside the cabin in the living room, the alien disguised as Joint stands by the fireplace looking at all the dead bodies that fill up the room. Bill and Danny are both dead and headless, Girl's also headless, and so is the real Joint. Mike is dead; he's missing both arms, and his head is cut completely in half. Patriot's dead; his face had melted off due to the creature's acid-like blood. He then smashed his skull to bits when he hit the cabin's floor face first. The creature of the night lays in the middle of the living room, split in two.

Blood, guts, bones, and pieces of brain are splattered on the floor, walls, and windows. The alien looks down at the real Joint's corpse and stares at it for a while. The alien sighs and then starts to walk out of the cabin. He steps over Bill's body, and before he can reach the exit, October pops up right in front of him. The alien disguised as Joint jumps, scared. The right side of October's face is swollen and smashed in a bit while the left side of her face is cut up and bloody with her left eye being the only one open.

"They are all fucking dead," October says quietly. She looks around and stares at all the bodies.

"October? Are you alive?" the alien disguised as Joint asks in excitement. He smiles as they both stare at each other.

"Joint, I can't really fucking see well. I have Danny's car key, but his tires have been slashed. I don't know what to do," October says.

She suddenly gushes blood out of her mouth. October holds up the car key with her left hand and quickly throws it at Joint. He catches the car key with his left hand before it landed on the floor. October's left eye suddenly zooms in on the catch, and she notices that Joint is missing his left-hand tattoo. She looks up, and Joint is staring her down. October backs up out of the cabin followed by Joint who is walking slowly.

"Buddy, it's over. We made it out alive," the alien disguised as Joint says, this time with his voice being distorted and echoing.

"You are not my friend! My friend is fucking dead on the floor!" October yells.

The alien smiles as he continues to walk toward October.

"Fuck off!" October yells.

She backs up and then trips, falling on her ass. She looks down at what she tripped on and sees that it's Mike's right arm. October looks up, and the alien is in front of her, smiling creepily.

"If you want to kill me, please just do it. But not as my friend, not disguised as him. Jason, what have they done to you?" October says, crying as she stares down the Alien disguised as her best friend.

The alien starts to cry. He holds out his untattooed left hand for October to grab so he can lift her back up. She shakenly grabs his left hand with both hands, and the alien lifts her back up.

"I didn't know. I thought I took the body of someone with low morals and a pointless life. But Jason or Joint, whatever you call that being, well we are both one. A part of him is still alive inside me, and I can feel all of his emotions, thoughts, memories, and pain," the alien says, backing up and then looking down at his left hand.

October looks at him confused.

"Even though I don't have the tattoo on my left hand, I can feel the pain from that day when he got it. Also I can't kill you. Jason won't let me. I can feel something between you two, more than some friendship bond. He loves you."

October falls to her knees crying. She continues to stare at the alien, this time with hatred. The alien walks forward and passes October.

"Where are you going?" October asks. She stands up quickly and turns around. The alien disguised as Joint has disappeared into the woods.

"Don't leave me like this! Don't fucking leave me, motherfucker! Joint!" October yells.

Silence is all she got back in return. October looks around, trying her best to see her surroundings, but she can only see what's in front of her, and it has to be close, otherwise it's a blur. She starts to panic and shake.

"Please don't leave me. Everyone is dead but me. I have no fucking clue on how I'm still alive, but fuck it, I'm alive. I just don't want to be alone," October says, speaking out loud. She continues to look around and sees nothing. No movement, no sound, no aliens, and no monsters.

"Hello?" October calls out. She looks around some more and then turns around. Still she finds and sees nothing. October turns to the left, and in front of her is an alien, all white with four black circular eyes. She stares at all four eyes as they are placed in the center of its face.

October suddenly gushes lots out of her mouth. Some of her blood lands on the alien's face. October looks down at her chest and sees that the alien has impaled her with a tentacle coming out from its right side. The white tentacle slowly exits October's chest, gutting her open from the right side. She watches as the tentacle combines itself to the alien's silky skin and disappears into it. October's vision becomes dizzy, and everything around her turns red. She drops to her knees and falls backward on her back, lying in the grass. The alien hovers over her and stares at her with a plan to strike and kill. October stares at the alien, and suddenly, her vision goes from red to blue and then red to blue. October watches as the alien's head suddenly explodes.

October watches as the headless alien falls to the ground dead. She smiles and looks up at the sky. October starts to think about everyone else. Mike, Joint, Patriot, Girl, Bill, and Danny are all dead. She remains as the last survivor of that night. That horrible night where everyone was murdered at midnight.

"Fuck! Is she alive?" a voice calls out. A man with short brown hair, long white beard, and wearing a police officer's uniform stands in front of October, looking at her. The officer is holding a pistol with both hands and is frantically pointing it at the woods.

"Joey! Call for the fucking backup! Call the fucking backup, Joey!" the officer yells.

October watches as the officer disappears from her vision when he moves toward the left. She hears the gun fire a couple times until it suddenly stops.

October continues to stare up at the sky smiling. Her vision turns gray, and she now hears nothing; it's just silence. October closes her eyes and sleeps peacefully. The sun shines, making the woods glow brightly. The woods in Idaho are peaceful and quiet with no sound.

About the Author

Justin Mead is a horror geek born and raised in Leominster, Massachusetts. As a teenager, he has always wanted to create something thrilling, whether it was creating videos or writing scripts. After high school, Justin started to write more. He ended up having to take a break due to personal events and work. One day, Justin was watching a horror movie with his mom, Gina. Justin and Gina disliked the movie. Justin knew that he could write something way better, so he dug through all his old scripts and found *Murdered at Midnight*. Justin then decided to write a book about it. Today, Justin continues his writing, being as creative and unique as ever.